SHARPAY'S FABULOUS ADVENTURE

The Junior Novel

Adapted by Ellie O'Ryan
Based on the Disney Original Movie, "Sharpay's Fabulous Adventure"
Produced by Jonathan Hackett
Executive Producer Ashley Tisdale
Executive Producers Bill Borden & Barry Rosenbush
Written by Robert Horn
Based on Characters Created for "High School Musical" by Peter Barsocchini
Directed by Michael Lembeck

DISNEP PRESS
New York

SHARPAY'S FABULOUS ADVENTURE

The Junior Novel

Chapter One

Standing on the polished stage, Sharpay Evans's heart pounded in time with the audience's thunderous applause. Hitting all the right notes, nailing all the right moves, watching a packed house leap to their feet and scream her name . . . it never got old. Sharpay grinned at her fans as she took a sweeping bow. This moment, in the bright, white-hot spotlight, was what she lived for. This moment made all those hours spent in auditions and rehearsals worth it—and then some. In fact, Sharpay rehearsed so much that her adorable little Yorkshire terrier, Boi, had learned all the moves, too. He barked happily next to her. Boi was just about the only performer Sharpay didn't mind sharing the stage with. After all, Boi was her very best friend.

After the curtain fell, Sharpay rushed into the lobby to greet her fans. It was never easy to get through the crowd after a show, but nothing would stop Sharpay from finding her two biggest fans: her parents. They were waiting for her with an enormous bouquet of roses.

"There's our little celebrity!" Mr. Evans announced. He wagged his finger at Sharpay. "Princess, you'd better look out for law enforcement. They might be coming after you for stealing the show!"

"Honey, on a scale of one to ten, you were on an entirely different scale!" Mrs. Evans exclaimed.

Everybody was laughing as Mr. and Mrs. Gonzalez, who were friends of Sharpay's parents, joined them. Standing next to them was a man Sharpay had never seen before.

"Sharpay!" Mrs. Gonzalez cried.

"Yes, I know," Sharpay said, batting her eyelashes. She was used to people complimenting her. "And thank you."

"We'd like to introduce you to Jerry Taylor," Mr. Gonzalez said.

"He's a good friend of our family, visiting for the week," Mrs. Gonzalez explained.

"May I say how *wonderful* you were?" Jerry commented as he extended his hand to Sharpay.

"As many times as you'd like!" Sharpay said brightly as she glanced over Jerry's shoulder. There were still lots of people waiting to congratulate her—and Sharpay didn't want any of them to leave before they had the chance.

"I really see a unique talent here," Jerry continued. "A true gift."

"And your kind, true words are a gift as well," Sharpay replied. "It was *so* nice to meet you, but if you'll excuse me, my friends have been waiting . . ."

Jerry smiled and handed Sharpay a business card. "I'm a casting agent," he said. "From New York."

"And my friends will keep waiting until I tell you how much I love your suit!" Sharpay exclaimed as her attention snapped back to Jerry. She tilted her head to make sure her best side was facing the casting agent.

"I'm about to start casting for a new musical on Broadway," Jerry told her.

Sharpay's eyes lit up with excitement. "Broadway?" she squealed. "As in . . . *Broadway?*"

"I think there's a perfect part. I'd be happy to arrange an audition if you should find your-self in the Big Apple anytime soon," Jerry offered.

Sharpay was so excited she could hardly speak. "That would be—! *I* would be—! *It* would be—!"

"The show is going to star Amber Lee Adams," Jerry revealed.

"*No!* Stop!" Sharpay shrieked. "*Seriously?* Stop!"

"Who is Amber Lee Adams?" Sharpay's mother asked curiously.

"She's *only* the most amazing performer ever!" Sharpay gushed. "We have so much in common!"

"Again, nice to meet you, Sharpay," Jerry said. "And congratulations. Who knows, maybe we'll see you in New York!"

Sharpay was too excited to respond, but the grin on her face and the sparkle in her eyes told Jerry everything he needed to know. Broadway . . . New York . . . the musical-theater capital of the world . . . The biggest dream Sharpay had ever had was about to come true.

And nothing and no one was going to stand in her way!

* * * * *

Except, maybe, one person.

Her dad.

"No," Mr. Evans said firmly. But he didn't look happy about it. Saying no to Sharpay was something he hardly ever did. Sharpay had been waiting for this opportunity her whole life. And now her dad was ready to kill that dream with one little word.

"*No*?" Sharpay repeated in amazement.

"No," Mr. Evans said again. "I don't think going to New York is a good idea."

"See, there you go believing everything you think!" Sharpay exclaimed.

"Do you really believe you're ready for such a monumental step?" Mr. Evans asked.

"Daddy, the main reason I buy such expensive shoes is so that I can *take* monumental steps," Sharpay replied as she admired her own gorgeous high heels.

"Sweetheart, when you graduated from high school almost a year ago, do you remember what you said to me?"

Sharpay frowned as she placed a perfectly

manicured finger to her lips. "How come no one makes a cap and gown in hot pink?" she guessed.

Mr. Evans shook his head. "No."

"How come you get a car and driver and I don't?" Sharpay guessed again.

"No," Mr. Evans replied patiently.

Suddenly, Sharpay's face lit up. "Good luck finding anyone to fill the talentless void of boring and unattractive people that will exist in these hallways once I graduate?" she remembered triumphantly.

"No," Mr. Evans replied before quickly correcting himself. "Well, yes, but you also said you needed one year to 'find yourself' and figure out what was next in your life. That year is about up, and you haven't found anything!"

"It's a small town!" Sharpay protested. "There's only so many places to look. Besides, I *did* find something. A show I want to be in."

"This isn't just *some* show," Mr. Evans said.

"You're talking about going alone to the big city."

"Right! To star on Broadway with Amber Lee Adams!" Sharpay exclaimed. "Could you really deny the world that opportunity?"

"I'm sorry, princess," Mr. Evans repeated. "But nothing you've shown me convinces me that you're ready for something like this."

Sharpay's dad leaned down and kissed her on the forehead. Then he turned and walked out of the room. Somehow, though, he missed the determined glint in Sharpay's eyes.

She had never given up on her dream before.

And she wasn't about to start now!

Sharpay immediately called her friends Tiffany, Lupe, and Dena—also known as the Sharpettes—and put them to work. While Sharpay occupied herself with a mani-pedi at her favorite salon, the Sharpettes made all her travel arrangements, rented a luxury penthouse for her, and booked an appointment at Jerry Taylor Casting. Sharpay was so thrilled that she then treated herself to a shopping spree! Then she spent half the night getting ready for the biggest performance of her life: convincing her dad to let her move to New York.

In the morning, Sharpay showed her parents the charts and graphs she'd made to prove how ready she was. She took a deep breath as she reached the conclusion of her presentation. "And *then* I'm a star!" she finished, grinning brightly at her dad.

But Mr. Evans shook his head. "I'm just not totally convinced."

"Daddy, you said I haven't shown you anything to let you know I'm ready for this," Sharpay said. "But look, I took matters into my own hands, and without even chipping my manicure!" She wiggled her fingers so her mom and dad could see her shiny pink nails.

"Hmm . . ." Mr. Evans murmured.

"But I've worked everything out!" Sharpay insisted. "*And* used this pointer."

"I don't know . . ." Mr. Evans said.

Sharpay was running out of options. It was time to get serious. "*Pleeeeeeease,* Daddy," she begged.

"Alone, in New York . . ." Mr. Evans replied. He looked worried.

Then Sharpay's mother spoke up. "You know, my dear college friend, Michelle, has a son that goes to NYU. I met him, he's a nice boy. I could ask her to have him keep an eye on you?"

Mr. Evans looked at Sharpay's impressive presentation again. "You really do think you're ready to take this on?"

"I *know* I can do this," Sharpay replied confidently. "I know it like I know purples wash me out, and that my eyes are the exact distance apart to be a supermodel. What I *don't* know is whether you believe in me. Mom seems to . . ." she said, her voice trailing off.

Mr. Evans looked at his wife and daughter as

they stared at him hopefully. There was only one thing he could say.

"Okay," he said with a sigh. "You have my blessing."

Sharpay shrieked as she hugged her dad. "Thank you, Daddy!"

"There's just one condition," Mr. Evans said loudly.

"Fine," Sharpay said. "I love a good conditioner."

But that's not what Mr. Evans meant at all. He gave his daughter a serious look.

"You have one month. I'll fly you to New York. I'll pay for a penthouse," he told her. "You just have to get in that show and prove you can be on your own. One month. Deal?"

"*So* deal," Sharpay replied, nodding.

"But, if it doesn't work out in *one month,* you come back and work for me, here at the country club," Mr. Evans said sternly.

Sharpay blinked as she tried to figure out what

her dad meant. "W—w—*work*?" she stammered.

"A job," he said firmly. "That's the deal. Prove yourself, or come back in one month and work for me."

"Fine. Prove myself it is!" Sharpay announced as she hurried off to her room to start packing. She wondered when the first flight to New York was. If she had only one month to prove herself, there wasn't a moment to lose!

Chapter Two

*A*fter a whirlwind of packing and hurried good-byes and a plane ride in first class, Sharpay arrived in Manhattan. As her sleek limo zoomed down the city streets, Sharpay stared out the window at the towering skyscrapers and bustling sidewalks. Everything about New York City was larger than life, and Sharpay couldn't wait to call it home—especially when the limo stopped in front of a luxury high-rise building! After making sure that Boi was safely tucked away in his designer carrying case, Sharpay stepped out of the limo.

A polished and professional-looking woman was waiting for her. "Sharpay?" she asked.

"In the flesh and pastels!" Sharpay announced as a doorman helped the driver unload her luggage.

"We spoke on the phone. I'm Marjorie Grande, the manager for the building," the woman said, introducing herself. "Please, follow me to the penthouse," she said, whisking Sharpay through the dazzling lobby to a private elevator that opened right into the fully furnished penthouse. The floor-to-ceiling windows offered such a breathtaking view that Sharpay gasped.

"I hope this is to your liking," Marjorie said.

"No, it's to my *loving*!" Sharpay squealed as she unzipped Boi's carrying case. "Boi, you *have* to see this!"

A frown immediately crossed Marjorie's face. "That's a dog," she pointed out.

"Try to get *him* to believe that!" Sharpay joked.

"I'm sorry. There are no dogs in the building," Marjorie informed her.

"Sure, there are," Sharpay replied as she gestured to Boi. "See?"

Marjorie shook her head. "The members of the co-op board have a *strict* no-dog policy."

"Well, my father heads our country-club board, so I'm sure that gives me some kind of board immunity," Sharpay said, thinking fast.

"Miss Sharpay, the building is pleased to have you," Marjorie said firmly. "This dog, not so pleased."

Sharpay looked around at the gorgeous penthouse, the steely determination on Marjorie's face, and Boi's beautiful brown eyes, which were staring into hers as he wagged his little tail. There was only one thing to say.

"Miss Grande, ma'am," Sharpay began, "if he goes, I go."

And that was all it took for Sharpay to find herself rudely ejected from the penthouse and out on the street. She clutched Boi close to her as people pushed past her, tripping over her pink luggage and shoving her out of their way.

What was she going to do now?

Suddenly, Sharpay realized that someone was filming her! She narrowed her eyes as she strode up to a guy with a camera. "Uh, what are you doing?" she demanded.

He lowered the camera just enough to reveal a handsome face and a playful smile—but Sharpay could tell from the blinking red light that the camera was still rolling. "Filming you," he replied. "Just keep doing what you're doing."

"Do you always just film totally stunning people on the street that you don't know?" she asked.

"Only when I think the subject is interesting," the guy said smoothly. "And you look baffled, and scared, and *really* pink. So yeah—interesting!"

"Are you paparazzi?" Sharpay asked, suddenly excited. She had expected to quickly become famous in New York—but not quite this quickly!

The cute guy laughed. "I'm a film student at NYU, working on a short film. The assignment is to capture one unique New York story. Maybe you're it."

"So you decided to film me without my permission, just for a school assignment?" she asked.

"Yup," he said.

"How *dare* you?" Sharpay snapped. "And my left side is better for close-ups." She tilted her head to make sure he was filming her from the best angle.

The guy grinned and stopped filming her for a moment. "I'm Peyton," he said, holding out his hand.

Sharpay glanced at his hand for a moment, unsure. Then she shook it. "Sharpay Evans. Actress. Heiress. Soon to be Broadway legend."

Peyton's eyes lit up. "Wait!" he exclaimed.

But Sharpay misunderstood. "About 105, but

it's really not polite to ask," she scolded.

"No," Peyton began, shaking his head. He tried to explain.

"I *should* know my own weight!" Sharpay cut him off.

"No, I'm Peyton Leverett," he told her. "Our moms went to college together. I was on my way up to your apartment to make sure you were okay. And here you are."

"Right!" Sharpay realized. "They told me to expect you. Glad we could finally meet."

Boi barked once in her arms.

"Oh, and this is Boi," Sharpay said.

"Nice to meet you, Boi," Peyton replied. "So, why are you out here? Is everything okay?"

"Not really." Sharpay sighed. "When I rented this apartment online, it never said they don't allow dogs. Now they won't let us live here. Well, it's their loss!"

"Do you have someplace else to go?" Peyton asked with concern.

"Okay, it's my loss *and* their loss," Sharpay admitted. "Actually, the only place I have to go is home. And trust me, that's not an option!"

Peyton was quiet for a moment. Then he had an idea. "Listen, there's an empty studio in my building, if you're interested. I'm friends with the building manager. I'm sure I could make a call," he offered.

For the first time since they'd met, Sharpay smiled. Peyton lifted the camera and started filming again.

"Well, since I don't seem to have any other options . . ." Sharpay said, glancing at her luggage. "Bellman!"

She looked from side to side, but no one appeared to carry her suitcases. That left just one option. Sharpay looked at Peyton with her eyebrows raised.

"Yeah, right." Peyton laughed. But he stopped once he realized that he was laughing alone. "Seriously?"

Sharpay smiled widely in response. She'd only been in New York for a short time, but she was certain about one thing: stars *definitely* didn't carry their own bags!

Just past the dazzling lights of Times Square and the vibrant marquees of Broadway's theaters, Sharpay and Peyton arrived at his building. It was small—about six stories—and made of brick. And it looked like it hadn't been renovated in ages!

Sharpay frowned. This building looked nothing like the luxury penthouse she had just left. Peyton, who was right behind her, was carrying all of Sharpay's luggage.

"Careful with those!" Sharpay called to him. "This is all I have to get by on until the truck arrives with the rest of my things."

Peyton set the heaviest bag on the sidewalk and wiped his forehead. "I finally understand why guys say pretty girls come with a lot of baggage."

But Sharpay wasn't listening. She had walked into the building's lobby—and what she saw horrified her. Sharpay screamed as she noticed the filthy floor and peeling paint.

"Oh, that's good!" Peyton exclaimed as he grabbed his camera. "Give me even more of that 'it's the end of the world' look!"

Sharpay tried to speak. But there were no words to describe this pit of an apartment building. Was this some kind of joke? How could anyone actually live here?

"Really," Peyton insisted. "You're going to love this place! Okay. Up we go!"

Sharpay glanced at the staircase, then back at Peyton. Surely, he wasn't suggesting that she climb the stairs?

"Oh, sorry," Peyton said. "No elevator. It's a prewar building."

"And during the war they didn't fight for an elevator?" Sharpay asked.

"The building has two things going for it,"

Peyton replied. "It's got something available, and *I* live here."

"Fine," Sharpay said. "But if I break a heel, *or* a sweat, you're responsible. Grab my bags." Cradling Boi in her arms, she climbed five flights of stairs.

"See? That wasn't too bad," Sharpay cooed to Boi, oblivious to Peyton's struggle with her heavy suitcases.

"Down the hall," Peyton panted as he leaned against the wall. "The one with the police tape and the chalk outline."

Sharpay's eyes widened.

"Kidding," Peyton said quickly. "About the tape."

Sharpay pulled a tissue out of her bag and used it to turn the doorknob. It took a few moments for her eyes to adjust to the dim light that filtered through two dirty windows. When they did, she couldn't believe how tiny the one-room apartment was. Or that there was a *bathtub* in the *kitchen*. Or that one of the windows faced a brick wall, while the other stared straight into somebody else's apartment. Sharpay spun around to face Peyton. "You said this was a studio!" she shrieked.

"It is," he replied.

"No way! MGM was a studio! This is a roach motel with no room service!" she cried.

"A studio *apartment*," he corrected her. "Sure, from certain angles it's a bit small. . . ."

"A two-karat engagement ring is small. *This* is a doll house," Sharpay groaned.

"So . . . what do you think?" Peyton asked.

"Forget it. I'd need an entirely separate apartment just for my lipsticks. And where I am supposed to sleep?" Sharpay wondered.

Peyton opened a closet to reveal a Murphy bed tucked inside it.

"*What* is *that*?" Sharpay asked.

"It's your bed," Peyton replied as he unfolded the convertible bed from the closet. When it

23

was fully set up, there wasn't even room to walk through the apartment.

"This is *not* a bed," Sharpay insisted. "You can't be serious!"

"Wait. There is one really good thing about it," Peyton said as he ducked out the door. The next thing Sharpay knew, Peyton was waving to her through one of the windows—the one that looked into a different apartment!

"See? This is my place! Looking better, huh?" Peyton said through the glass.

Sharpay yanked open the window. "Am I missing something? Oh, right. Space! Luxury! Maid service!"

Peyton frowned. He walked back into the studio. "Let me guess. You're used to being spoiled."

"I'm not *used* to it. I just expect it," Sharpay replied.

"You know, half this building is filled with performers who came here with the same ambitions you did," Peyton said. "What makes you so much better than them?"

Sharpay counted the reasons on her fingers. "Money. Breeding. Talent. Great hair. Perfect jawline. Chic taste. How much time do you have?"

Peyton shut off his camera. "Fine. Go. I tried to help you out like my mom asked, but whatever. I'll find someone else to film."

"The problem is, if I call my father and tell him how I messed up on the other apartment and how I have nowhere to go but *here,* then I ask for help, he'll make me come home and . . . w—w—work!" Sharpay exclaimed.

"*So?*" Peyton asked.

"*So*? Then I'll *never* get my break." She shot Peyton a look. "And promise you won't call your mother and tell her about this, because then she'll call my mom, who will tell my dad, and I don't think he really believes I can make this happen. He only gave me one month to prove it!" she cried.

"Then you've got one month to prove it," Peyton replied.

Sharpay started walking in a small circle, thinking about what she should do. Without missing a beat, Peyton turned the camera back on.

"Why did I do this?" Sharpay asked herself. "I want my canopy bed and my housekeeper and a bathroom that doesn't share a sink with the kitchen."

Peyton nodded toward the door. "Come on."

"Where?" Sharpay asked.

"Do you trust me?" Peyton replied.

"You suggested *this* place," Sharpay reminded him.

"Point taken." Peyton grinned. "Come anyway . . ."

Sharpay scooped up Boi just as Peyton grabbed her hand and pulled her out of the apartment. Somehow he managed to film Sharpay as he guided her through the bustle of the crowded streets.

"Where are you taking me?" Sharpay asked.

"You'll see," Peyton replied mysteriously.

Within minutes, they stood in front of the doors of a theater. Sharpay watched curiously as Peyton texted someone. Suddenly, one of the doors swung open. "Let's do this!" an artistic-looking guy announced.

"Do *what*?" asked Sharpay. "What are we doing?"

But no one answered her, and the guy ushered them into the theater. In the darkness, Peyton positioned Sharpay in the exact center of the stage.

"Hit it, Butchy!" Peyton called to the guy.

The theater was instantly illuminated by hundreds of dazzling lights. Boi started to bark excitedly.

Sharpay gasped. "Wow,"she said. She was in complete awe.

Peyton caught it all on camera—Sharpay's wide eyes, her enormous smile, the shine of her hair in the spotlight. Sharpay clutched Boi tightly as she realized that she was standing on an actual Broadway stage. It was overwhelming.

Peyton could relate. "I know," he told Sharpay. "When I left Indiana to go to school here, I didn't know a soul either, and I was just as overwhelmed as you. But I had two things: my dream and my camera. And look at me now!"

"You *still* only have your dream and your camera," Sharpay pointed out.

"Yes," Peyton acknowledged. "But I met you, didn't I? So, something's working out."

"Well, *whenever* people meet me, things get better," Sharpay said with a grin.

"You just have to adapt to your surroundings and remember that for now, this is all just temporary," Peyton said.

"*Right*," Sharpay replied thoughtfully. "Like prom dresses and first boyfriends."

"Anything you have to do will be worth it to get your dream," Peyton told her.

Sharpay's eyes gleamed. "I'll meet with that casting director, get the part, be a star, and have a palace!" She paused. "Well, a suite at the Palace Hotel." She looked directly into Boi's eyes. "We can do this!"

"There you go," Peyton said. "*That's* the self-indulgent, self-entitled, optimistic pink hurricane I've been seeing through my lens!"

"And I like how perceptive you are," Sharpay replied. "Okay, New York. Bring it on!"

Whatever Sharpay had to do to make her dream come true, she was ready to do it!

Chapter Three

$\mathcal{T}$he next few days were a whirlwind of new experiences for Sharpay and Boi, including their first hot dog from a street cart (yuck!) and their first encounter with a giant roach (double yuck!). But it wasn't all bad. One afternoon, they stumbled upon a talented group of street performers and joined in the show. Another time, they discovered a fabulous boutique that stocked *only* pink items! Sharpay found everything she needed there to remodel her new apartment in just her style. And that's how, little by little, the city started to feel like home.

One morning, Sharpay woke up with her heart pounding: the big day had arrived. She dressed herself and Boi in adorable matching outfits, then opened the blinds to let in some light. Peyton saw her and started filming through his window. "Are you on your way to meet with the casting director?" he called.

"No, I'm on my way to change theater history!" Sharpay declared. She twirled around. "You think this is a good outfit for changing history?"

"Perfect," Peyton replied. "Mind if I tag along and film? Not that you could ever mind me, right?"

"I think you should," Sharpay agreed. "After all, not many people can say they were there to film the birth of a legend!"

Full of confidence, Sharpay and Boi strutted outside and walked to the theater, with Peyton and his camera trailing behind them. Though the theater was crowded with hopeful actors waiting to audition, it didn't take long for Sharpay to find Jerry. He recognized her right away. "Sharpay! You made it after all!" he called.

"Destiny called, and I get great reception!" she replied.

"Your timing is perfect," Jerry said. "What's tomorrow like for you?"

"The first day of the rest of my fame," she joked.

"I'll set your audition for three o'clock and e-mail you the musical number you should do," Jerry said as he shuffled through a stack of headshots. "And, of course, make sure he's well-groomed and, you know, takes care of business beforehand."

Sharpay blinked. "What?" she asked, confused.

"What?" repeated Jerry.

"*He*?" Sharpay asked, not sure she had heard correctly.

"Yes," Jerry said.

"Wait . . . *what?*" she asked again.

"It's your dog we want to audition," Jerry explained. "He was amazing. I sent you the information in response to your e-mail. Didn't the title of the musical give you any indication? *A Girl's Best Friend*?"

"Yes. *A* Girl's *Best Friend*," Sharpay said. "And I'm here for the *girl.*"

"You're here for the *girl*?"Jerry asked, surprised.

"Well, I'm never the best friend," Sharpay informed him.

Jerry shook his head. "No. We wanted Boi."

"As the girl?" Sharpay asked in disbelief.

"As the best friend," he said.

"Wait," Sharpay said once more as everything become suddenly, horribly clear. "You wanted *Boi* as the best friend of the girl, not *me* as the girl with the best friend?"

"Exactly," Jerry replied

"Let me explain," Sharpay said quickly. "If I

don't star in this show, I'll have to go back home and work for my father. Starring on Broadway is *so* much better."

"I'm sorry for the confusion, Sharpay, and if you don't want Boi to audition, I totally understand," Jerry said sincerely.

Sharpay couldn't think of a single thing to say. She tried to stay calm as she walked out of the theater. But once she hit the street, she started running.

"Slow down!" Peyton yelled. "Even New Yorkers can't keep up with you!"

"It's not even me they wanted!" Sharpay cried.

"To be fair, the role is for a *dog*." Peyton tried to comfort her. "If they wanted *you* I could understand being upset."

"Why did I come all this way?" Sharpay wailed. "Leave my friends, my family, a dry, self-hydrating climate?"

"To follow your dream—or at least that's what

I thought," Peyton reminded her, still filming. He was capturing some real emotion.

"Nothing is turning out the way I planned!" Sharpay cried. "Plan A, live in a penthouse and star on Broadway. Plan B, uh, don't *have* a Plan B! What do I tell my father now?"

"That you came to a very special city determined to be someone very special . . . which you are," Peyton replied.

Sharpay looked up at him as a shaky smile crossed her face. "Oh, I'm not so special," she said. "I'm just like everyone else, maybe a little better."

"Look at it this way," Peyton said. "Boi is your dog, and he has an opportunity, so be happy for him."

Sharpay paused. "You're right. I'm being . . . what's that word? When you do something for yourself even though it's not so good for other people?"

"Selfish?" Peyton guessed.

"No," she said. Then she thought for a moment. "Oh. Yeah."

"Sharpay, you can't give up," Peyton told her. "And anyway, you're officially the star of my film."

"I *am*?" she asked in surprise.

"Yeah. You are," he told her.

"Oh, so now it's all about you?" Sharpay said playfully.

"Only because I need you here!" Peyton exclaimed.

"Fine, I'll star in your movie," Sharpay said, starting to feel like her old self. "Okay, change of strategy."

"I didn't know you had a strategy," Peyton teased, "but I like the way you think."

"Okay . . . if Boi becomes a success, everyone will see me as well," Sharpay continued. "After all, I *am* his entourage. I *am* the one who holds his leash. His fame will ultimately lead to my fame, and that's what I came here for, right?"

"Still a little selfish, but heading in the right direction," Peyton replied.

"We're going to do this!" Sharpay said excitedly. "They want Boi to audition? It's Boi they will get!"

With a look of determination on her face, Sharpay scooped up her dog and set off for her apartment. Boi had some moves to learn before his audition, and Sharpay was going to make sure he was perfect!

*   *   *   *   *

The next day, Sharpay and Boi took the stage confidently. Their performance was as fantastic as Sharpay had hoped, and the entire creative team burst into applause when the routine ended. Two men rushed toward the stage.

"I'm Gill Samms, the director," one man said.

"Neal Roberts. Writer," the other man added.

"That was amazing!" Gill told Sharpay.

"Boi was *meant* for Broadway," Sharpay said. "We both were. So, when do we start?"

Just then, the stage manager walked over to them. "There's one more waiting," he said.

Sharpay and Boi reluctantly left the stage as a twelve-year-old boy walked out from the wings. By his side pranced a prim King Charles spaniel.

"Roger Elliston the third," announced the stage manager, "and his dog, Countess."

The boy smiled. "As you can see by our extensive resume, hand-printed on carbonless, environmentally friendly rice paper," Roger began, "Countess has numerous major Broadway credits under her paws, including *The Collar Purple, Three Puppy Opera,* and the original Broadway cast production of *A Wagging Tail of Two Cities*, a musical opera. In German."

"*Major* pedigree," Gill said, marveling.

"I'm impressed!" Neal exclaimed.

"Plus, she can bark a high C, with sustained vibrato," Roger added.

"Sure, but only dogs can hear it," cracked Sharpay.

As everyone laughed, Roger shot Sharpay a dirty look. "Let's see what Countess can do," Gill said.

As Roger and Countess began their routine, Sharpay watched with a growing sense of unease. Could this little pipsqueak and his furball actually be competition? As soon as the song ended, everyone in the theater clapped and cheered wildly—except Sharpay.

Gill and Neal turned to face the audience. "Amber Lee? What do you think?" called Gill.

"Yes," said Neal. "Amber Lee? Thoughts?"

From the darkest recesses of the theater, a beautiful young woman appeared. It was Amber Lee Adams, Sharpay's celebrity idol!

"We are *so* meant to be BFFs," Sharpay whispered to herself. She quickly fluffed her own hair, then Boi's.

"There's our little star," Gill beamed.

"*Big* star," Neal said. "What did you think?"

Amber Lee climbed the stage and stood next

to Roger. "Wow! Wow is a word, right? Wow!"

Then she turned to Sharpay. "But *your* dog. Also, wow!"

"I know, right!" Sharpay exclaimed. She ran onto the stage with Boi, pushing Roger out of the way. But to Sharpay's surprise, Boi started barking at Amber Lee—and not in a friendly way.

"He's just saying hi," Sharpay said, trying to cover for him. "Sharpay Evans. Of the New Mexico Evanses. I'm a *mega*fan!"

"Are not!" Amber Lee replied.

"*So* am," Sharpay said.

"I'm going to tweet about you right now!" Amber Lee announced as she grabbed her phone.

Sharpay checked her phone and squealed in excitement. "She did! She tweeted!"

"Okay, I don't know how we'll decide," Amber Lee continued as she turned to Roger. "You're amazing."

"All this, *and* a grade-school diploma," Roger said proudly.

Then Amber Lee turned back to Sharpay. "And *you*!" she said, clearly impressed.

"Will you tweet that?" Sharpay asked.

"Just did," Amber Lee replied. "I'd be excited to work with either of you and your dogs."

"Well, I know both these talented dogs want to work with you, too," Gill said. "But only one can be in the show."

"How can we choose?" Amber Lee asked.

"Wait. How about we work with both dogs during rehearsals?" suggested Neal.

"Wait," Amber Lee said, as if a thought had suddenly dawned on her. "How about if we work with both dogs during rehearsals? Then I can see which one I work best with!"

"I think it sounds like a solution," Gill replied.

"We have a solution, people!" Neal announced.

Sharpay looked at Roger. Roger looked at Sharpay. Neither one was pleased as they stared at each other with narrowed eyes.

Their dogs, however, felt differently. It was

clearly puppy love at first sight for Boi and Countess. And now they would get to spend every day together!

As Amber Lee walked toward the lobby, Sharpay scurried after her. To Sharpay's delight, Amber Lee turned to her and smiled. "Can I just say how totally great you are?" Amber Lee began.

"You do, and I'll never wash my ears again!" Sharpay joked.

"Know what *I* think?" asked Amber Lee. "Well, of course you don't because I just thought it . . . but I think they loved you!"

"I like the way you think," Sharpay replied, totally flattered.

"You're such a good singer, too," Amber Lee continued. "And I should know. My album went triple platinum."

"Well, I've done quite a bit of theater," Sharpay told her.

"It shows," Amber Lee said. "I'm going to have my assistant give you my number. If you need anything, you let me know. We girls have to stick together."

A shy girl stepped forward to hand Sharpay a slip of paper.

"Wow," Sharpay said in amazement. "This is actually your number. It looks like any ordinary number, but it's not ordinary. It's yours."

Amber Lee smiled. "And, hey, may the best dog win!" Amber Lee added as she walked away. Sharpay looked down at the slip of paper in her hands. She was *beyond* excited.

Outside the theater, Peyton was waiting for her with his camera rolling.

"Can you believe it?!" Sharpay squealed.

"You were great," Peyton said. "Boi was great!"

Sharpay picked up Boi and gave him a big hug. "This new strategy just might work," she said happily.

"I think Amber Lee really liked you, too," Peyton added.

"Is she awesome or what?" Sharpay exclaimed

happily. "She inspires me. There. I said it. We are *so* going to get that part!"

"How do you know?" Peyton asked.

"Easy," Sharpay said with a shrug. "I don't do rejection."

The theater doors swung open as Roger and Countess sauntered outside. "Sharpay," Roger said, "I just wanted to wish you both luck."

"That's very nice," Sharpay said pleasantly.

"*And* suggest that you give up now while you still have your dignity, distant though it already might be," Roger finished with a smirk.

Sharpay raised her eyebrows. "Sorry, which Smurf are you again?"

"True, you have talent," Roger said, "but you lack both the experience *and* the finesse to ever achieve this holy grail of possibility," Roger said.

"Yeah, but Boi is cuter," Sharpay shot back.

"Countess is a theatrical ninja," Roger retorted.

Sharpay pretended to doze off. "Sorry, for a minute there you bored me to death."

But Roger wasn't done. "I have a foolproof strategy for getting what I want: See it. Want it. Have a fit. Get it."

"Yeah, well, this playdate's over," Sharpay snapped.

"I hope you enjoy rejection!" Roger told her.

"We're *going* to get that part," Sharpay said.

"*We're* going to destroy you," replied Roger.

"Bring it on!" Sharpay challenged.

"Oh, it's *brought*," Roger said coldly. Then he turned around and walked away. Countess ran after him, sneaking one last glance at Boi. Boi barked lovingly. Sharpay, on the other hand, crossed her arms with a huff. She—and Boi—*had* to get this part.

Chapter Four

$\mathcal{S}$harpay and Boi spent the rest of the day rehearsing in their apartment. "We are *so* ready to take them on," Sharpay told Peyton with a satisfied smile. "And look," Sharpay directed Peyton to her dog, "all Boi can do is think about how horrible that other mangy little dog was."

But from the longing, love-struck look in Boi's eyes, it seemed that Sharpay was wrong.

"If you want success so badly, then you'll get it," Peyton said as he filmed. "All you need is one shot to make it happen."

"And this is my shot!" Sharpay exclaimed.

"Doing this is all I ever dreamed about, especially since I already have everything else."

"Well, there's still humility," Peyton joked.

"What's wrong with being confident?" Sharpay asked, checking her reflection in the mirror.

"Confidence is when you know you're good," Peyton explained. "Arrogance is when you *think* others know you're good."

"Well, I want everyone to know I'm as good as I think everyone *thinks* I am without them knowing I know they think it," Sharpay replied. "And do you have to film *everything*?" she added.

"Yup," Peyton said without missing a beat. "Because this is *my* shot. If my professor loves my film, he talks about it, then there's a buzz, then it's in a festival, then it gets distribution, then I'm signing a studio deal, then I'm getting an Oscar."

Sharpay couldn't help but smile. She recognized the look in Peyton's eyes. "So, you always knew you wanted to make films?"

"It kind of started when I was a kid. A substitute teacher would show movies," Peyton explained. "Everyone goofed off, but I thought: how would I have filmed that differently?"

"Really?" Sharpay asked. "I knew I wanted to be an actress the first time I produced and performed the entire production of *Snow White*—musical numbers, full dance, handmade costumes," Sharpay said. "Everyone in that preschool worshipped me!"

They laughed again. "I just want to spend every day waking up and being onstage," Sharpay said wistfully.

As she glanced out the window at the city lights sparkling against the night sky, Sharpay truly hoped that tomorrow would take her one step closer to making her dream come true.

*   *   *   *   *

Soon it was time for Sharpay and Boi to go back to the theater. As they arrived, Gill's voice boomed loudly. "Welcome to the first rehearsal—"

"Of the new Broadway musical—" Neal interrupted.

"*A Girl's Best Friend!*" Gill finished.

The first three rows of the theater were filled with the show's cast members, including Amber Lee, of course. Sharpay and Boi—and Roger and Countess—were there, too, eyeing each other suspiciously. At least, Sharpay and Roger were. The two dogs wagged their tails happily as they exchanged a glance across the aisle.

"You're all amazing," Neal said. "And heading up our superb cast, we are thrilled to welcome one of the biggest stars around, Amber Lee Adams."

As everyone cheered, Amber Lee stood up and smiled sweetly. "Can I just say, this is the chance of a lifetime for me. Broadway's not like TV or movies—because on Broadway, people can see if you write your lines on your hands!"

Everyone laughed adoringly.

"All right, let's rehearse!" Gill announced. "I want everybody downstairs with piano, rehearsing the music for the opening number. Amber Lee and Judith, I want you onstage so we can block the first scene. Why don't we start with Boi?" Amber Lee and Judith nodded. Judith would be playing Amber Lee's mother in the play.

On cue, Boi trotted onto the stage carrying an envelope in his mouth. Beaming with pride, Sharpay silently applauded as Boi performed without missing a single cue! And best of all, Gill and Neal seemed delighted with him.

"Okay, let's get Countess in there. And continue," Gill called.

"Prepare for artistry!" Roger sneered to Sharpay.

To Sharpay's dismay, Countess did a great job, too. Sharpay hated to admit it, but Countess was almost as talented as Boi. *Almost.*

When the scene ended, everyone applauded.

"And both dogs—great work!" Neal commended them.

Sharpay and Roger stared at each other from opposite ends of the theater. Sharpay knew that she would do anything—well, *almost* anything—to make sure Boi got the part. And she could tell that Roger felt the same way.

But what Sharpay didn't know was that for Roger, "almost" didn't apply.

Before rehearsal the next day, Roger snuck into Amber Lee's dressing room. After making sure that no one was looking, he rubbed a piece of chicken all over Amber Lee's shoes! An evil smile crossed Roger's face. Now it was up to Boi to take the bait.

When Boi walked onstage to rehearse with Amber Lee, he couldn't resist her chicken-scented shoes! Sharpay was horrified when he started chewing on them!

"I'm sorry, what's going on?" Amber Lee asked, disgusted.

"All right, get me the other dog!" Gill yelled frantically. They couldn't have a dog acting so unprofessionally!

Humiliated, Sharpay hurried onstage to get Boi. Her sweet little dog *never* acted like that. Then she noticed Roger's smug grin. Her eyes narrowed.

"Sorry," Roger said, shrugging—but he didn't sound sorry at all. "What can you do?"

Sharpay didn't reply. If Roger wanted to play dirty, she'd have to up her game.

At rehearsal the next day, Countess trotted over to Amber Lee. Suddenly, the little dog stared into the theater, whining and howling. Something was *really* bothering her.

"Gill!" Amber Lee called.

"Roger, figure out what's going on with the dog," Gill snapped. "Meanwhile, get the other dog."

Roger looked at Sharpay suspiciously, but she just smiled as she tucked a dog whistle into her pocket. "Sorry. What can you do?" she said with a shrug.

But Roger wasn't about to back down. At the next rehearsal, he snuck a cat into the theater— and let it out in the middle of Boi's scene! Boi dashed after the cat and accidentally knocked down Amber Lee. Then the stage manager lunged for Boi, setting off a crazy chase: the yowling cat tore through the theater with Boi racing after it, the stage manager desperate to catch them both.

"Okay, everyone!" Gill cried, frustrated. "That's ten!"

As the cast and crew took a break, Roger strolled past Sharpay. "I'll admit it. You're good," he said in a low voice. "But we're better. Give up."

"Give up?" Sharpay asked. "Not until there's a Broadway marquee with a picture of my dog so big you can walk by it and smell his puppy breath!"

Before Roger could reply, the stage manager

approached them, carrying Boi under his arm. "I have to take the dogs for a nap," he said. "Union rules."

Roger and Sharpay stared at each other with loathing as Roger handed Countess to the stage manager. Backstage, the pups snuggled into their beds, clearly too exhausted to cause any more trouble.

"Awww," Amber Lee said as she spotted the dogs.

"Pretty cute, huh?" asked the stage manager as he hurried off to take his break.

"Hi there, sweeties," Amber Lee cooed. Then she shut the door—and her smile vanished. "So, I just wanted to let you know—this is *my* show. *I'm* America's sweetheart. *I'm* the one they're paying to see. Not you two overbred furballs. So, until I can figure out a way to get rid of you, watch your step, or you'll find out the *real* meaning of going home in a doggie bag."

Plastering a phony smile across her face,

Amber Lee slipped out of the room, leaving Boi and Countess alone. The two dogs exchanged another glance, but this time there was more than puppy love in their eyes.

They looked absolutely terrified!

*   *   *   *   *

That evening, Sharpay and Peyton sat together in Sharpay's apartment working on their laptops. Well, Peyton was working. He was editing his movie. Sharpay was online shopping. But, hey, that was hard work, too!

"This film is cutting together really well," Peyton commented, stretching his arms behind his head.

"Do I look amazing?" Sharpay asked.

"The camera loves you," Peyton replied.

"I know!" she said with a grin.

Then a look of panic crossed Sharpay's face as she heard her computer beep. "Oh, no! My dad's video-chatting me! He thinks I'm in a penthouse. I can't let him see that I'm living in a tiny studio.

In a filthy tenement. With a *boy* in my room! A boy, by the way, that has no money and lives in a *tinier* studio, and who has apparently *never* heard of the words 'maid service.' No offense."

"What of that could possibly offend me?" Peyton asked.

Suddenly, he had an idea. "Come with me!" Peyton grabbed Sharpay's hand and pulled her toward his own apartment. He positioned Sharpay in front of the window, which had an amazing view of the city skyline. Sharpay perched on the radiator and turned the laptop to face her. All her dad would see was his darling little girl with the big city behind her. Sharpay took a deep breath and accepted her father's video chat.

"Hi, Daddy!" Sharpay chirped.

"Hi, princess," Mr. Evans said. "How's my little girl?"

"Overpaying for everything and yelling at total strangers," replied Sharpay.

Mr. Evans laughed. "You're practically a native! Where are you? The view is spectacular."

"Oh, well, there's hardly a penthouse in the city that doesn't have a spectacular view," Sharpay replied airily.

"And are you the toast of Broadway?" her father asked.

"I've been busy . . . with rehearsals," Sharpay said quickly. It wasn't a total lie.

"Wonderful!" Mr. Evans exclaimed. "You got into that show?"

"Well, it doesn't quite work like that," Sharpay admitted. "It's . . . complicated. But I know it's going to work out." She gave her father a wide smile.

"Sharpay, is there something you're not telling me?" Mr. Evans asked. "Remember our deal. If things aren't working out—"

"I know, I know," she interrupted. "I have one month to get in this show, and then—"

"Two weeks," Mr. Evans corrected her. "You

have two weeks left. Sharpay, are you sure every-thing's all right?"

"It's fine, Daddy!" Sharpay insisted, hoping he would be convinced.

"Well, okay," Mr. Evans sighed. "We miss you, honey. I love you. Now, how the hootie do I turn this thing off?"

Sharpay watched her dad fiddle with his computer. Suddenly the video-chat window disappeared, and she breathed a sigh of relief. Then her face filled with worry.

"Boi *has* to get that role! I can't go home!" she cried. "Not as a failure. I need some sort of subtle, visibly crushing advantage over Roger." Sharpay looked at her perfectly manicured nails and sighed.

"Why not just trust Boi is talented, that you've trained him well, and let fate take it from there?" Peyton suggested. He put his hand on Sharpay's shoulder.

"Fate?" Sharpay asked. "I can't trust fate.

Some matters you just take into your own hands." She twisted around on the radiator and stared out the window at the glittering city.

All she needed was one idea—one *really* good idea—to guarantee Boi's Broadway debut. There had to be something that Sharpay could do. Now if she could only figure out what it was!

Sharpay was thrilled that a casting agent from New York had asked her to audition for a Broadway play!

"You have one month. You have to prove you can be on your own," Sharpay's father told her.

Sharpay was one step closer to fulfilling her dream when she arrived in New York City.

Since her penthouse apartment didn't allow dogs, her new friend Peyton offered her a studio in his building. It was far from glamorous.

The role in the Broadway play was actually intended for Sharpay's dog Boi instead of her!

"You were great!" Peyton told Sharpay after she coached Boi through his audition.

Sharpay prepared Boi for his stage debut!

Amber Lee Adams, the star of the show, made quite an entrance.

"Bad news! My maid quit. Here's a list of chores," Amber Lee told Sharpay.

Sharpay was glad to have met Peyton.

Boi and his new friend Countess had run away!

"At first, I idolized you even more than myself. But
you're not at all what I thought you were,"
Sharpay told Amber Lee.

Boi was ready for showtime!

It was opening night of the play—starring Sharpay!

Sharpay's Broadway dreams had come true, and they were better than she could have imagined!

Chapter Five

$\mathcal{B}$efore rehearsal the next day, Amber Lee sat in her dressing room fuming. Everything in the room was beautiful—except, at that moment, Amber Lee. Her face was twisted into a horrible scowl as she yelled at Kelly, her assistant. "What do you mean you 'forgot' my bottled water!"

Kelly took a deep breath and tried to explain. "I was rushing to get those magazines you wanted from across town when I was knocked down by a bike messenger, so I stopped at the hospital for, like, one second to get some stitches—"

But Amber Lee wasn't listening. "And meanwhile, I had no water!"

"I can get it for you now?" Kelly said hopefully.

"*Now* I've had to drink tap!" Amber Lee yelled.

"I'm sorry," Kelly apologized. "I'll do better."

"Forget it," Amber Lee said icily. "You're of no use to me. You're fired!"

Kelly's eyes filled with tears. Choking back a sob, she ran out of the room just as Sharpay came down the hall. Sharpay's eyes widened when she saw how upset Kelly was. She decided to poke her head in Amber Lee's dressing room to find out what was going on.

"Amber Lee?" Sharpay said.

Amber Lee smiled brightly at Sharpay. All traces of her temper had vanished. "Wow, you look so cute, Sharpie!"

Sharpay tried to correct her—politely. "Shar*pay*."

"Oh, you changed it?" Amber Lee asked. "I

like that even better. So, what's on your mind?"

"I was just walking by and I saw your assistant leave in tears," Sharpay explained.

"She's not my assistant," Amber Lee said, rolling her eyes. "She quit."

Sharpay nodded understandingly. "No wonder she was crying."

"I don't think she even cared," Amber Lee replied. "Next time I should probably just hire a best friend instead."

Sharpay's eyes lit up as she had an idea. Not just any idea—a *great* idea. One that might push Boi into the spotlight. "Wait!" she exclaimed. "Are you thinking what I'm thinking?"

"What are you thinking that I should be thinking?" Amber Lee asked.

"I could help you out until you replace her!" Sharpay exclaimed.

"That *is* what I was thinking about thinking," Amber Lee said, shocked.

"Of course, this can't in any way affect your

choice of which dog gets the starring role," Sharpay said innocently.

"Oh, it won't," Amber Lee assured her.

"I couldn't live with myself if I thought I did anything unfair," Sharpay continued.

"You have my word," Amber Lee promised. "Hey! I know. How about dinner?"

"That sounds awesome!" Sharpay replied.

"Right? Get me a reservation for two at someplace fantastic. Then call my agent and have her meet me."

"Oh," Sharpay said, trying to cover her surprise—and her disappointment. "Sure."

Amber Lee reached forward and grabbed Sharpay's hands. She turned on her most dazzling smile. "I won't forget this! And I promise you, it won't be because you're helping me out *if* I happen to take an extra liking to Girl."

"Boi," Sharpay corrected her.

"Oh. You changed it," Amber Lee said. "I like that even better! And could you please take my microphone back to the sound person, and tell him or her the wire hurts my scalp."

Amber Lee shoved the mic pack into Sharpay's hands with an extra smile of gratitude. Sharpay hurried out of the dressing room, thrilled to have the chance to help her idol.

But the minute Sharpay was out of sight, Amber Lee made a face of disgust. Then she poured hand sanitizer all over her palms.

Sharpay found the sound engineer checking the settings on the soundboard. She held out the mic. "Amber Lee says the wire is hurting her scalp. Personally, I think she uses the wrong shampoo, but she's the star and—"

"Your mic. It's hot," the man explained. "It means it's on. When this switch on the mic pack is flipped, it's on, and it goes through the entire theater."

Sharpay's mouth dropped open in horror. She spun around to see that everyone was looking at her. "You could have led with that part, thank you," she whispered fiercely. Then she leaned close to the mic and announced, "Amber Lee's got a *great* scalp!"

Sharpay shoved the mic pack into the sound engineer's hands and scurried off. Her first task as Amber Lee's assistant didn't go quite so well!

*   *   *   *   *

That night, Peyton filmed Sharpay while she told him all about her conversation with Amber Lee.

"Then she asked me to help her out after her assistant quit, and after I suggested it!" Sharpay said excitedly.

"Are you sure this is wise?" Peyton asked. "I'm sorry, let me rephrase that: this isn't wise."

"It's perfect," Sharpay argued. "Amber Lee will see that she and I are exactly alike, we'll become BFFs, she'll make sure Boi gets the role, then his fame becomes my fame! This is the advantage I've been waiting for."

"Isn't it more like *taking* advantage?" Peyton replied.

Sharpay ignored him. "And my father thought I couldn't do this in a month!" she exclaimed triumphantly. "It's turning out better than I imagined!"

Behind the camera, Peyton was not convinced. He wanted to warn Sharpay again, but he could tell from the grin on her face that she wouldn't listen to anything he had to say.

*   *   *   *   *

Several hours later, Sharpay was deep in sleep when her cell phone started ringing. She peeled the cucumber slices off her eyes and tried to turn on the light and answer the phone, all at the same time.

"Hello?" she mumbled into her phone. "Sure, be right over."

Still bleary-eyed, Sharpay got dressed. On her way out the door, she noticed that it was two o'clock in the morning. Her beauty sleep was ruined, there was no doubt about that. But if Amber Lee needed her, Sharpay wasn't going to let her new friend down.

Minutes later, Sharpay arrived at Amber Lee's gorgeous penthouse apartment. She found Amber Lee in her enormous closet, pointing at a shoe box on a high shelf.

"I can't reach that!" Amber Lee whined.

Sharpay blinked. Had Amber Lee really dragged her out of bed in the middle of the night to fetch a *shoe box*? She shot Amber Lee a look that said *seriously?* and repeated, "Can't reach it?"

Amber Lee had seen that look before. She acted fast. "Okay, this was kind of a test," she said. "Only a true friend would have come here at this hour and do this."

Sharpay's annoyance melted away at the words *true friend*. "So, I passed?" she asked.

Amber Lee merely smiled in response as Sharpay reached for the box.

* * * * *

Only a few hours later, Sharpay found herself back at Amber Lee's apartment, helping the star get ready for a busy day of being famous. She stifled a yawn as a sleek black limo arrived to pick up the star. "And don't forget your photo shoot," Sharpay reminded her.

"You're a *life*saver!" Amber Lee exclaimed. "You *must* be at the shoot with me to make sure I look flawless, like *you* always do!"

"Are you serious?" Sharpay asked.

"Serious?" Amber Lee said. "You are *now* also my stylist! Teach me all your secrets! Gotta go!"

Sharpay watched the limo pull away, a huge smile plastered on her face. It had only been one day since Amber Lee's old assistant had quit— and now Sharpay and Amber Lee were practically best friends! And, Sharpay realized, it was still early enough that she might be able to catch a catnap before Boi's rehearsal.

But Sharpay quickly found out that napping was not an option. Amber Lee kept Sharpay so busy with errands that she didn't even have a chance to sit down until that evening. And when she did, it was only to do work for Amber Lee. Sharpay sat with a highlighter in her hand and script pages spread all around her. Just then, Peyton poked his head into Sharpay's apartment. "How about dinner?" he asked. "Split some egg rolls at Wok This Way?"

Sharpay barely glanced up from the script. "Can't. I have to highlight these script changes for Amber Lee, then highlight her hair. *Highlight* of my night!" she joked halfheartedly.

"Okay, but I miss spending time with you," Peyton said, looking at her from the doorway. "And you did promise to shoot some more stuff for my film."

Lack of sleep and the pressure of a packed day pushed Sharpay over the edge. "You know, what I'm doing is important, too!" she snapped. She ran her fingers through her hair in frustration.

"Whoa," Peyton said, holding up his hands as he stepped back into the hall. "For a minute

there, you sounded like Amber Lee." He gave
Sharpay a disappointed look. He turned and left,
but his words kept running through Sharpay's
mind. She frowned in frustration.

For some reason, Peyton had made that sound
like a bad thing.

Chapter Six

$\mathcal{A}$ny hopes Sharpay had of catching up on sleep the next day were lost after Amber Lee gave her a dozen more tasks. By the time Sharpay arrived at the theater for rehearsal, she had circles under her eyes that were so dark, they required concealer to cover them—and Sharpay had *never* needed to use concealer on her flawless skin. She tried to smile as she let herself into Amber Lee's dressing room while carrying the star's dry cleaning and all her bags. Amber Lee was waiting for her.

"Bad news," Amber Lee said immediately.

"My maid quit. So, here's a list of chores."

"*Chores*?" Sharpay asked incredulously. Sharpay Evans did *not* do chores.

"And I wanted to talk to you about Boi," Amber Lee added, sensing Sharpay's hesitation. "But you have to swear it'll stay between us."

"Okaaaaaay," Sharpay said slowly, wondering if this was the moment she'd been waiting for.

"Well, I think I'm going to tell the director to give Boi the part," Amber Lee continued.

"Seriously?!" Sharpay gasped.

"Almost positive," Amber Lee said, nodding.

"You won't be sorry!" Sharpay cried.

"Trust me, I know," Amber Lee replied, giving Sharpay a big hug. Then she handed Sharpay the list of chores.

As Sharpay looked over the list, her face went pale. She braced herself for what promised to be a miserable day . . . but one full of learning experiences. Like learning how to work a washing machine. And learning how to make a protective suit out of trash bags so she could scrub a toilet. As she held the toilet brush in a perfectly manicured hand, Sharpay paused. Was *any* dream worth something this gross?

She sighed, nodded, and went back to work. After all, she *had* vowed to do almost anything to make her dream come true.

But what Sharpay hadn't realized was that Amber Lee's housework would keep her away from the theater all day.

During a break, the stage manager gave Roger a stack of pages. "There are some changes in blocking for the dog scene, top of Act Two."

"Countess can learn them in no time," Roger replied. "She has a memory like a digital hard drive. No bark and all megabite."

"I need to find Sharpay and make sure she gets them," the stage manager said. "Boi is doing the first run-through tomorrow."

"I'd be more than happy to deliver them," Roger said innocently. He snatched the pages and walked out of the theater before the stage manager could respond. Once he was in the back alleyway, Roger pretended to glance around—as if Sharpay liked to hang out in smelly, grimy alleys. "Sharpay?" he whispered.

There was no response—and Roger didn't expect one. He slunk over to the Dumpster and, glancing around again, tossed the script pages into it. "Aww, now that's unfortunate!" he said gleefully.

* * * * *

The next day, Sharpay was so grateful to be back in the theater—and not scrubbing a toilet—that she could hardly wait for rehearsal to begin, even if she wouldn't be onstage.

"Life is so strange." Amber Lee was reciting her lines to Tim, the actor playing her boyfriend. "Shelby and I travel halfway across the country to find fame and fortune, and instead we find love."

"Lenore, I have something to ask you," Tim recited. "*We* have something to ask you. . . ."

Boi knew his cues perfectly. At that moment, he ran from stage left and prepared to jump into Amber Lee's arms.

But what Boi didn't know—thanks to Roger—were the blocking changes—and he accidentally slammed into Amber Lee, knocking her down! Everyone gasped as Amber Lee and Boi fell to the stage in a heap. Sharpay raced down the aisle to help her dog.

"He's supposed to come on from the other side with the ring!" Amber Lee yelled.

"Sorry," Gill apologized. "We changed that blocking. What happened?"

"What's the problem with this dog?" Amber Lee said, so harshly that everyone turned to stare. She quickly tried to cover up what she had just said. "And make sure he's okay," she added sweetly. "It's not his fault. He's just a dog."

Gill sighed. "Okay, let's all break for a few."

Amber Lee turned on her most charming smile, but the rest of the cast and crew didn't respond. They'd seen enough of her real personality to know when she was being phony.

As Sharpay picked up Boi, the stage manager approached her. "I don't know what happened," Sharpay began.

"We sent out new script changes, but Boi didn't do them," the stage manager replied.

"But I didn't get any new . . ." Sharpay said in confusion.

The stage manager, however, didn't care. As she watched him walk away, Sharpay noticed Roger in the front row, grinning smugly at her.

"I looked everywhere last night to give them to you," he said. "I guess working for Amber Lee has its drawbacks."

"You did this on purpose!" Sharpay hissed.

Roger pretended to look shocked. "That's a complete—yeah," he admitted, enjoying himself immensely.

Boi and Countess exchanged a worried glance and tried to push their owners apart.

"You're threatened because you know Amber Lee's going to choose Boi," Sharpay said.

"Not after today she won't," Roger replied smugly.

"Countess doesn't have *half* the personality that Boi has," Sharpay said hotly.

"And Boi doesn't have half the talent that *Countess* has," Roger shot back. "Isn't that right, girl?"

When Roger looked down for Countess's approval, he realized that she was gone—just as Sharpay noticed that Boi had disappeared.

"Countess?" Roger cried.

"Boi?" Sharpay called.

Sharpay and Roger exchanged worried glances. Without another word, they raced across the stage, through the lobby, even going down to the basement, but their dogs were nowhere to be found.

"Maybe they went out back!" Sharpay suggested breathlessly. She and Roger raced outside, but the alley was deserted. With shaking hands, Sharpay called Peyton. "Boi and Countess are gone! We have to find them!"

"*Gone*?" Peyton asked into his phone. "Wait, where are you now?"

"Leaving the theater," Sharpay replied as she charged over to the sidewalk, with Roger on her heels. "We're going to look around here. Can you look near the apartment, in case they come back?"

"Of course," Peyton said. "Keep me posted. I'll meet you back at the theater."

As Sharpay hung up, she turned to Roger. "What if they were dognapped?" she asked, terrified.

"Do you think we pushed them too hard?" Roger asked. "Countess is übersensitive. She cries watching dog food commercials!"

"I just hope they're not huddled in a corner somewhere, afraid, lost, at each other's throats!" Sharpay cried.

But Sharpay's and Roger's fears couldn't have

been further from the truth. Boi and Countess were enjoying a dream date in one of the most romantic cities in the world! After a horse-drawn carriage ride through Central Park, the two pups frolicked in a stream of water coming from a fire hydrant. They saw breathtaking views of Manhattan. And when a menacing Rottweiler tried to catch Countess's eye, Boi growled so fiercely the big bully knew right away that Countess was taken.

For Sharpay and Roger, though, the evening passed by in agony. Sharpay was so scared she completely forgot that Roger was her enemy. Right now, he was the only person in the world who could understand how terrified she was. "What if we never see them again?" she asked, on the verge of tears.

Roger put his arm around Sharpay and tried to comfort her. "They're smart dogs," he said. "Smarter than we are. They'll be okay."

Just then, they heard a familiar bark!

Sharpay looked up, hardly daring to hope that her precious little dog was back. What she saw seemed almost too good to be true: Peyton was rounding the corner, carrying Boi and Countess!

"Countess!" Roger shouted.

"Boi!" cried Sharpay.

"It's amazing," Peyton said with a grin. "They came back to the apartment."

Everyone hugged as they celebrated the dogs' return. Then Roger scooped up Countess. "Thanks, Peyton," he said gratefully as he turned to leave. "Oh, and Sharpay . . . it's still on."

"Bring it," she replied.

But they exchanged a knowing smile, and Sharpay had a feeling that there wouldn't be any more dirty tricks.

*   *   *   *   *

Back at her apartment, Sharpay sat Boi down for a serious talk. "You bad, bad boy, Boi," she said sternly. Then she scooped him up in a hug. "I'm just glad you're okay."

"He and Countess had an adventure," Peyton said, sitting down next to her.

Sharpay frowned. "She probably coaxed him to join a doggy gang or something," she sniffed. "We'd better check him over for tattoos."

"Are you so lost in what you're doing that you haven't noticed?" Peyton asked.

"Noticed what?" Sharpay asked.

"Boi and Countess are in love," he replied.

"With *what*?" Sharpay asked.

"Each other," he said, laughing.

"No way!" Sharpay cried. She held Boi in front of her face and gazed deep into his eyes. She gasped. "You're right! He's dilated. He's got . . . puppy-dog eyes. How could I not have noticed puppy love?"

"There's a lot you haven't noticed," Peyton said quietly. "Like, lately, you've had no time for me. I was counting on you to help me finish my film."

"I said I would and I will," Sharpay said

defensively. "Things have become complicated."

"It's not that complicated," Peyton said, disagreeing. "Amber Lee is using you, and you're letting her."

"You don't know what you're talking about," Sharpay replied.

"I *don't*?" asked Peyton. "Where's the Sharpay that was determined not to go back home because she didn't want to work for anyone?"

"Why don't *you* tell *me*?" Sharpay said, her eyes flashing angrily.

"Working for someone, that's where," Peyton replied. "So at least be honest as to *why*."

"I know what I'm doing!" Sharpay insisted.

"You've sold your soul to get Boi in that show, rather than trust in the dog you raised," Peyton said. "Even worse, you've stopped trusting that your own talents would get you where you need to go."

Sharpay's temper flared. "And maybe *you're*

jealous because I'm on my way up with a new famous friend, and you're just a student making a film about someone else's life instead of your own!"

Sharpay regretted the words the moment she'd said them, but it was too late to take them back. Peyton stood up, clearly hurt. "You don't have to be in my movie anymore. I get it. You have more important things to do."

"Fine," Sharpay said. She watched Peyton open the door and step into the hallway. Then he turned around.

"One question," Peyton added. "What happened to that hot pink whirlwind of confidence and ambition I saw through my lens that first day you got here? That girl *knew* she was special. That girl knew she didn't have to do any of this to succeed. What happened to her, huh?"

Then Peyton walked away, leaving Sharpay in stunned silence. She shook her head, trying to figure out what had just happened—and trying to forget the awful truth in what Peyton had said.

She didn't have to dwell on their fight for long: at that moment, her cell phone rang. It was Amber Lee with yet another urgent request. For once, Sharpay was happy to rush over to her apartment. It was better than sitting home reliving her argument with Peyton.

"Oh, and Sharpay, can you make sure as many people as possible from my fan club get invited to the first-night dress rehearsal?" Amber Lee asked. "I want that theater filled with people who love me as much as you do."

Sharpay stifled a yawn. "Sure," she replied, as she signed Amber Lee's name to a stack of head shots.

"Hey, you know what sounds great after all this work?" Amber Lee said suddenly. "A long, luxurious spa bath."

"It sounds amazing!" Sharpay exclaimed, shaking out her tired wrist. "Thank you!"

"Run one for me, will you?" Amber Lee

requested as she stood up. "And then finish these. You're the best!"

Amber Lee dropped another stack of head shots in front of Sharpay, then skipped off to her bedroom. When she was sure that Amber Lee was out of earshot, Sharpay sighed heavily.

Being Amber Lee's friend and assistant was officially not as great as she'd imagined it would be.

Chapter Seven

Sharpay tossed and turned all night, still too upset from Boi's disappearance—and her fight with Peyton—to get any sleep. She wished for a chance to explain that she hadn't meant what she'd said, but Peyton kept the window to his apartment covered. The message was clear: he didn't even want to see her.

After what had happened with Peyton, Sharpay was determined not to let anything hurt her new friendship with Amber Lee. She couldn't lose her only other friend in New York. So she decided to impress Amber Lee by finishing her errands before rehearsal. Walking down the dimly lit hallway to the dressing rooms, Sharpay could hear voices arguing inside Amber Lee's dressing room: Amber Lee, Gill, and Neal. It was clear right away that something was wrong—very wrong.

"I don't think you're hearing me!" Amber Lee yelled.

"New *Jersey* is hearing you!" Gill shot back.

Kindhearted Gill sounded angrier than he ever had before. Sharpay pressed her ear against the wall and listened.

"The show is called *A Girl's Best Friend*," Neal said patiently.

"I didn't say change the *title*!" Amber Lee replied.

"But you want the 'best friend' written out!" Neal pointed out.

"Oh. Right." Amber Lee shrugged. "Change the title."

"How are we supposed to get rid of one of

the main characters a *day* before our dress rehearsal in front of an audience?" Gill asked incredulously.

"People are coming to see *me*," Amber Lee said frostily. "You reduce that dog's part to a bark, or I don't go on."

"Let's be reasonable . . ." Neal pleaded.

"I'm a star, I don't *have* to be reasonable." Amber Lee cut him off. "Those dogs are bugging me almost as much as those two disposable owners. I had to have one of them clean my toilet just to keep her away. She thinks she's an actress. Right! She *acts* just like every other obsessed fan."

Sharpay sucked in her breath sharply as her eyes filled with tears. She could hardly believe her ears.

But as much as she wanted to run from the theater, Sharpay forced herself to stay. She blinked back her tears until she was calm enough to face Amber Lee without saying exactly what she thought of her. Because, Sharpay realized, Peyton was right. She'd come to New York to follow her dream, and she wasn't about to let anyone stand in her way.

Especially not Amber Lee Adams.

* * * * *

When rehearsal ended, Sharpay and Boi slipped out quietly. On the way home, Amber Lee's words kept running through Sharpay's mind, until she was just as angry as when she'd first heard them.

As she approached her building, Sharpay saw Peyton walking out the door. He stopped briefly and gave her an awkward smile. Then he continued on his way.

"Wait," Sharpay called after him.

Peyton turned to look at her.

"Everything you said," Sharpay began. "You were . . ."

"Right?" guessed Peyton.

"Yes," she admitted.

"Thank you," he said quietly, and the gentleness in his voice made Sharpay burst into tears. In an instant, Peyton was by her side, wrapping her in a hug.

"You must think I'm a total fool," she said, wiping her eyes.

"Nah," Peyton replied. "Not total."

"Maybe my dad was right," Sharpay said, as she stared at the sidewalk. "Maybe I'm not ready for this and should go work for him. I mean, did I really think I was just going to come to Broadway and be a star?"

"Yes," Peyton said firmly. "Because that's exactly how you think. And it's perfect."

"Perfection is so hard!" Sharpay sighed. "And it doesn't prepare you for disappointment."

"Well, if it helps, you still look adorable, even when you're disappointed," he told her.

Sharpay thought for a moment. Then she shook her head. "Yeah. That doesn't help."

As her eyes filled with tears again, Peyton

cupped her face in his hands. He lifted her chin so that he could look directly into her eyes. "Sharpay, there's not a marquee big enough or lights bright enough to contain the fame you're going to have."

Just the thought that someone else out there believed in her helped Sharpay find her confidence. "But not the way I've been doing it," she realized. "Like you said, the Sharpay you know isn't the Sharpay that has become the Sharpay that is *this* Sharpay."

"Did all the Sharpays follow that?" Peyton grinned.

"I sacrificed integrity for opportunity! I let someone insecure distract me! I cleaned a bathroom!" Sharpay said indignantly. "But, worst of all, I disappointed someone I care about and forgot what is really important to me. I lost track of what I want."

"And other than maid service and a canopy bed, what is it you want?" Peyton asked.

"A fair fight," Sharpay replied, her eyes glittering with determination. "And maybe you'll let me still be in your movie."

Peyton's smile was all the answer she needed.

* * * * *

When Sharpay and Boi arrived at the theater the next morning, Countess was waiting for them. She catapulted through the lobby toward Boi, the stage manager charging after her. Sharpay saw how eagerly Boi wagged his tail. "Fine. Go," she said, smiling.

With an excited yip, Boi galloped over to Countess and the two dogs started running in happy circles, pausing only to touch noses. Sharpay grabbed her cell phone and sent an urgent text. Then, turning the dogs over to the stage manager, she hurried to the basement.

Moments later, Roger met her there. "I got your text. What's 'CQMTWILGT'?"

"'Come quick. Major trouble. Wow, I look great today.'" Sharpay translated for him. "Duh."

95

"I really should have gotten that," Roger replied, shaking his head.

Sharpay took a deep breath. "Amber Lee Adams isn't what you think," she announced.

"A self-absorbed, two-faced panther who would eat her young live on a reality show rather than allow anyone to steal her spotlight?" Roger asked.

"Okay, she's what you think," replied Sharpay.

"Listen, I don't care if her parents had to tie beef jerky around her neck just to get the family dog to play with her, as long as Countess is at her side on that stage," Roger said.

"That's what I'm trying to tell you!" Sharpay exclaimed. "She wants the part of the dog written out completely!"

It took Roger a minute to understand the full implications of what Sharpay had said. But when he did, he was furious. He pitched an *enormous* tantrum. He stamped his feet. "Not fair!" he screamed, his face turning red.

"Roger, we've been fighting the wrong battle—

against each other," Sharpay told him. "We need to form an alliance and work against a common enemy."

"But what can we do?" Roger asked hopelessly.

"Tonight is the dress rehearsal," Sharpay began. "The audience will be filled with members of Amber Lee Adams's fan club."

"I know, I saw the tweet," Roger replied.

Sharpay looked at him curiously.

"Fine, yes. I follow her, too!" he admitted.

"We need to show people *exactly* who Amber Lee really is," Sharpay continued. "It's time someone taught her a lesson about how to behave in the theater!"

"I like the way you think. It's manipulative but for a good cause. Tell me what you need me to do," Roger said, and Sharpay leaned close to whisper her idea.

* * * * *

It was less than an hour until curtain time, and Amber Lee was totally frazzled. Her hair was perfect. Her costume was perfect. Her makeup was perfect. Even her mic pack was perfect. But Sharpay was nowhere to be found.

The moment Sharpay strolled into her dressing room, Amber Lee pounced. "I've been trying to call you all day!" she snapped.

"Oh. Sorry, my phone must have been turned off," Sharpay said casually.

"Without asking me first?!" Amber barked.

"Good luck tonight!" Sharpay replied. "I know you chose Countess to do this performance. I'm fine with that."

Amber Lee shrugged. "It's not personal, but your phone was off so I couldn't talk to you about it. Guess that won't happen again, will it?"

Sharpay forced herself to nod understandingly. "We're good. Hug?"

Amber Lee half-nodded, so Sharpay leaned forward to hug her, trying not to cringe with loathing. The hug was essential to Sharpay's big plan—because reaching around Amber

Lee's back let her turn on the mic pack.

And Amber Lee would never notice.

As Sharpay hurried out of Amber Lee's dressing room, she knew that the entire cast and crew were full of jitters. But as her heart started pounding in her chest, Sharpay was sure that no one else could possibly be as nervous as she was.

For Sharpay, the stakes were much higher than forgetting a line or missing a cue.

The theater was packed. Every seat was occupied by a member of Amber Lee's fan club—except for the one in which Peyton sat. The quiet murmurs of the audience dropped to a hush as Gill and Neal stepped in front of the curtain.

It was almost showtime!

"We are *thrilled* you're here for our first performance in front of an audience!" Gill announced.

"Does everyone here know how to applaud?" asked Neal playfully.

Behind the curtain, there was complete silence as the actors took their places. Sharpay stood just offstage in the wings. Directly across from her, Roger held Boi and Countess. Their eyes locked, and he waited for the signal.

Suddenly Amber Lee arrived, shoving people out of her way as she stormed onto the stage.

Sharpay nodded at Roger. This was it. He carefully placed Boi and Countess on the floor, and the little dogs scampered up to Amber Lee! They started dancing around her, nipping at her dress and shoes.

A look of disgust crossed Amber Lee's face. She tried to push the dogs away, but that just riled them up even more. "Someone control these wannabe werewolves," she ordered. "This is *exactly* why I didn't want to do a show with dogs! *I'm* the star! Not them!"

What Amber Lee didn't realize was that her mic was on—and every word she said boomed through the theater, amplifying her nastiness so that everyone could hear it. Gill and Neal dashed behind the curtain to find out what was wrong.

"Can't someone put these rats with rabies out of their misery?" Amber Lee snapped.

The stage manager rushed onstage to corral Boi and Countess. Briefly, he caught Sharpay's eye; she winked at him and opened the curtain, so that Amber Lee's fan club members could see her true self. But with her back to the audience, Amber Lee didn't notice that the curtain was up.

The stage manager scooped up Boi and Countess and held them away from Amber Lee.

"Finally, you idiot!" she yelled. "What took so long? Now, hurry up and get these four-legged fleabags out of here! There are people out there waiting to see me! You think all those boring freaks with no lives came to worship two no-name mutts? *I'm* the one they love! Me! They came to see . . ."

As she turned to take her place on the stage,

101

Amber Lee suddenly realized that the curtain was up. The audience—her fan club—had seen her. And they'd heard every word.

As Neal had suggested, they knew how to clap.

But, they also knew how to boo.

The sound of hundreds of people booing echoed through the theater until it was so loud and so overwhelming that Amber Lee had to run from the stage. On her way out, she almost knocked over Sharpay and Roger.

"I knew I forgot to tell you something," Sharpay said. "Careful, your mic's on."

"You did this! You've ruined me!" Amber Lee shrieked, throwing her mic to the floor in anger.

"News flash—*you* ruined you!" Sharpay replied.

"What do *you* know?" Amber Lee shot back. "You're a nobody! The only reason you wanted to be my friend was so I'd pick your dog."

"No," Sharpay said, shaking her head. "At first, I idolized you even more than myself, which isn't easy! But you're not at all what I thought you were."

"You and I are *exactly* alike," Amber Lee said.

"Except I don't enjoy letting people down," Sharpay said. "I don't use people to feel better about myself. And I definitely don't wear yellow and orange in the same week, let alone in the same outfit. Maybe I *did* think you and I were alike, but not anymore. In fact, I'd be embarrassed if someone thought I was like you."

"Well, I quit. Without me, there's no show. Neither of your frizzy fur balls will get their chance now," Amber Lee announced. Then she faced Sharpay. "And neither will you!" Amber Lee's chin jutted out as she waited for someone to beg her not to quit the show.

But no one did.

"Blame *her*!" Amber Lee shouted, pointing at Sharpay

As Amber Lee stormed away, everyone turned to Sharpay.

"I'm sorry, but someone had to say it," Sharpay told them.

Gill buried his head in his hands. "I'll go talk some sense into her," he said, groaning. Then he turned to Sharpay. "*You*! Out of this theater. And take your dog, too!"

Sharpay's eyes filled with tears as she scooped up Boi. If her plan had worked so well, why did she feel so awful? Before she reached the door, Roger ran up to her.

"Sharpay, if you go, I'll go, too," he said loyally.

Sharpay shook her head. "No. You wanted this as badly as I did," Sharpay told him, smiling through her tears. "This mess was my idea. You win."

"That's not what it feels like," Roger replied. He reached up to give Sharpay a hug. Then Sharpay slipped out of the theater as Boi and Countess exchanged a look of longing. Sharpay squeezed Boi tightly as she walked along the busy streets where no one even noticed—or cared—that tears were streaming down her face. She felt completely defeated.

It was time to face the fact that she had failed. It was not easy to face.

And it was time to say good-bye to her dream.

Chapter Eight

The golden sunlight that streamed into Sharpay's apartment the next morning seemed too cheerful for such a sad day. Boi, clearly unhappy as well, curled up in his dog bed while Sharpay began packing her things. For such a small studio, she'd managed to squeeze a lot of stuff into it.

A knock at the door interrupted her. She found Peyton standing on the doorstep. "Hey. Can I come in?"

"Sure," Sharpay said quietly, opening the door wider.

He immediately noticed the suitcases. "So, you're really leaving?"

"Yeah." Sharpay pointed at the stack of luggage by the wall. "I'm packing my carry-on stuff first."

"I wish you weren't going," Peyton said.

"Me, too," Sharpay replied.

"Have you thought about what you're going to do now?" Peyton asked softly.

Sharpay shrugged. "Move home ·where there's enough room for my pores to open, spend months in the spa getting this layer of New York grime off my skin, and mostly . . . miss you."

"I know exactly how to help that," Peyton announced. "Don't go."

"I already talked to my dad," Sharpay replied, looking away. "I guess I'm going to start w—w—"

"You don't have to say it," Peyton interrupted. He knew how hard it was for her to face the idea of working. "What about your dream of becoming a star?"

"It's still there," Sharpay said. "It's just a little bit more of a dream than a reality. You know what today is?"

"What?" Peyton asked.

"I got here exactly one month ago. My time was up tonight anyway."

"So you still have . . ." Peyton checked his watch. "Eight hours!"

Sharpay's smile was full of sad resignation. Eight hours wasn't enough time to change anything.

"This isn't how my movie is supposed to end," Peyton continued.

"I guess it is," Sharpay said with a sigh.

Suddenly, Sharpay's cell phone rang. "This is Sharpay. Oh, sure. No, I'll be there." She hung up and turned to Peyton. "That was the stage manager. They want me to come to the theater and clear out Boi's things."

"I can go with you if you want," Peyton offered.

"I want," Sharpay replied.

She reached for Boi.

Peyton reached for her hand.

And together, the three of them set off for one last walk to the theater, where Sharpay's dream had seemed so close to coming true. The theater was oddly quiet and it didn't take them long to find the stage manager, who was waiting in the wings to help them pack up. The entire cast— except for Amber Lee—had assembled in the first two rows of the house.

"And so, Amber Lee has quit," Gill told everyone.

"The producers feel, without a star, we can't open," Neal said.

"The time it would take to find someone who could learn the role, and do it well, might be weeks," Gill explained. "And it would cost too much to keep the production going."

"But we want you all to know, it was great *almost* working with you," Neal said sincerely.

Boi started barking, and everyone turned to

look at him. Sharpay couldn't bear to see the looks of disappointment and frustration on their faces. She whispered to Peyton, "I'll meet you outside." Then she tucked Boi under her arm and hurried down the long aisle toward the exit.

"Thank you all for your hard work, people," Gill finished. "We are so sorry."

"Wait!" a voice suddenly shouted.

Peyton's voice echoed through the theater as he jumped off the stage, landing right in front of the actors. "It's not over. I mean, it doesn't have to be!"

Peyton grabbed his laptop. In the back of the theater, Sharpay watched from the shadows as Peyton loaded a video clip he'd shot of Sharpay and Boi. Late one night, after everyone else had gone home, they had snuck into the theater to practice—and Peyton had filmed every minute of it.

"You're perfect," Sharpay told Boi on the video.

Boi performed a trick and barked happily.

"I love when you use that accent!" Sharpay cooed. "But shhhh, we're not supposed to be here."

The cast laughed, and a small smile flickered across Sharpay's face.

In Peyton's film, Sharpay sat in the center of the stage. "Okay, now let's do the scene where the character of Lenore thinks she has lost everything, and you come over and nuzzle in her lap to help her feel better. I'll do Amber Lee's part, except with actual acting."

The actors laughed again, and this time Gill and Neal joined in, too.

Sharpay began to recite Amber Lee's lines. "Oh, Shelby, what is going on? I feel like I'm invisible here. Nothing is working out. . . ." Sharpay took a deep breath and began to sing, putting her whole heart and soul into the performance.

At the end of the song, the entire cast burst into applause, cheering so loudly that Peyton had to shout—"Well, did I tell you?"—just to be heard over them. He ran down the aisle and pulled Sharpay out of the shadows.

"Amazing!" Gill exclaimed.

"Amazing!" Neal echoed.

"You have more depth, range, and tone in one note than Amber Lee had in her entire body," Gill declared. "The producers will love it!"

"Wait," Sharpay said, hardly daring to believe her ears. "What are you saying?"

"We need you to save the show!" Gill cried.

"Seriously?" She gasped.

"We know it's a risk . . ." Neal began.

"And true, we *did* fire you," Gill added. "But now I'm *un*firing you. We need you!"

"What do you say?" Neal asked Sharpay.

Sharpay glanced from face to face, until her eyes met Peyton's. He smiled at her knowingly.

"I guess we could take the costumes in a few sizes and get everyone used to hearing the songs sung on key, but there's one condition . . ."

Sharpay said slowly. "Boi and Countess split the role of Shelby the dog. Equally."

"Done!" Gill announced.

Neal clapped his hands. "We have a lot to do, people."

"Let's rehearse!" Gill announced.

The cast scurried onto the stage to take their places, but Sharpay hung back. She stood very close to Peyton as she whispered, "Thank you."

"This is it!" he said excitedly. "The chance you've been waiting for!"

"What if I'm not ready for this?" Sharpay asked.

"Oh, you're ready," Peyton said confidently. "*Ready* isn't as ready as you are."

"But what if I'm horrible?" Sharpay wondered.

"Won't happen," Peyton told her.

"What if I forget my lines?" she remarked.

"Impossible," he said.

"What if—" she began.

But this time, Peyton cut off Sharpay before she

114

could voice any more of her fears. "Everything in your life so far has been leading you to this moment," he said. "*Your* moment. Embrace it!"

Instinctively, Sharpay leaned into him, facing the fear pounding in her heart. "I'm scared."

"Finally," Peyton said, knowing how hard it was for Sharpay to admit it.

"One week to opening night!" Gill's voice rang out. "Let's go, people!"

Sharpay took the stage, smiling at Peyton over her shoulder as he grabbed his video camera.

Their dreams were waiting for them.

And Sharpay and Peyton were ready to make them come true.

*   *   *   *   *

The week passed by in a blur of late-night rehearsals, last-minute costume fittings, and more singing and dancing than Sharpay had ever done in her life. Suddenly, it was *her* name in lights on the marquee; *her* parents dressed in the fanciest clothes they owned finding their seats in the front row with Peyton; and *her* chance to star on Broadway.

Opening night had arrived!

As the paparazzi snapped thousands of photos, a parade of limos pulled up in front of the theater, and everyone who was anyone in the New York theater scene arrived for the premiere performance of *A Girl's Best Friend*—and the debut of Broadway's newest star—Sharpay Evans!

But from backstage, Sharpay wasn't a part of any of the craziness. She stood calmly, quietly, waiting for the moment when the curtain would rise. Then she heard it:

Tap-tap-tap.

The conductor's baton struck the music stand.

The orchestra was at the ready.

The show was about to begin.

As the curtain rose, Sharpay reveled in the warm glow of the spotlight. The band began to play.

And Sharpay began to sing.

Her heartfelt song filled every corner of the theater, captivating the audience. She could tell as she performed that everyone was blown away. Under the sparkling lights, Sharpay was radiant. This was it: her chance, her moment, her dream coming true.

And it was better than she had ever imagined!